In every generation there is a Chosen One. One girl in all the world. She alone will stand against the vampires, the demons, and the forces of darkness. She is the Slayer.

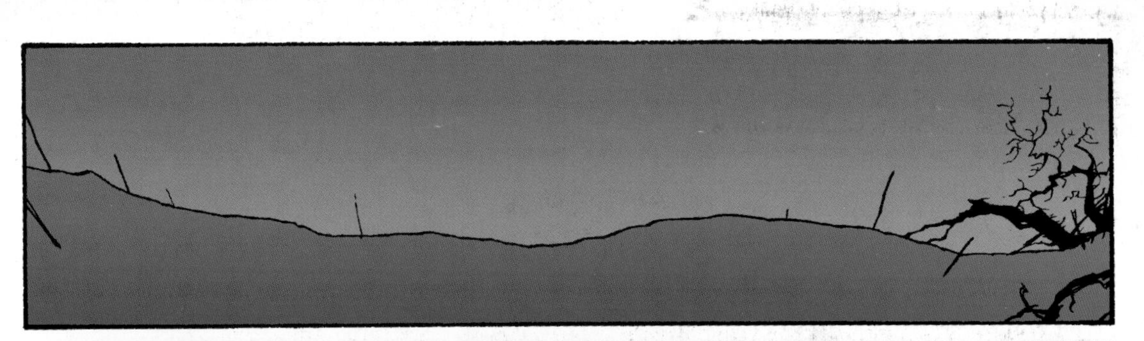

I AM ALONE.

THERE IS THE FIGHT...
BUT IT WILL BE BRIEF.

THERE IS THE BEAST....

... BUT IT WILL BE DUST.

THEY WILL BE GONE, AND I WILL ONCE AGAIN BE A--
EXCUSE ME ...

I HAVE BEEN SENT TO YOU. PLEASE DO NOT BE ANGRY AT MY INTRUSION. I BRING GIFTS, FOOD AND SUPPLIES FROM THE VILLAGE.
OUR ELDERS THANK YOU FOR SAVING US FROM THE DEMONS...

... AND ASK THAT YOU LEAVE.

THEY SAY YOU ARE PART DEMON.

THEY SAY THE SHADOWMEN MADE YOU BORN WITH DEMON INSIDE AND THAT IS HOW YOU ARE ABLE TO FIGHT THE VAMPIRES.
THAT"S WHY THEY FEAR YOU.
WHY THEY CH-CHOSE ONLY ONE.
THEY SAY THAT WHEN YOU DIE, THERE WILL BE ANOTHER GIRL CHOSEN. AND THEN ANOTHER, FOR ALWAYS. AND YOU WILL BE IN THEM AND THEY IN EACH OTHER AND YOU WILL NEVER DIE.

I WANTED YOU TO KNOW OF THAT ...

OTHERS.

THE THOUGHT FILLS ME WITH FEELINGS I HAVE TO STRUGGLE TO NAME.
CONFUSION. PITY. COMFORT.
THERE WILL BE OTHERS...

...LIKE ME.
TALES OF THE SLAYERS
A YU, VINES JOINT.

I found her first at evening prayer
Inside the small stone church
So shoulder-stooped, so wan with care,
The object of my search
She would not heed my tale at first
I'm told it's often so
She neither fought nor cried nor cursed
She simply answered, "No."
Just "No." -- and turned -- I ran behind
To ask, "How can you know?"
INRI

"For God is good, and God is kind
And would not curse me so."

RIGHTEOUS

But she could not for long deny
The power in her veins
She said, "Christ suffered -- so shall I
To thank him for his pains."
And so she trained; she studied, fought,
Preparing for her war
She soaked up all that could be taught
and still desired more
No longer pale, but flush with life
She strengthened every day
Young men, on hunt to find a wife
Surprised, looked oft' her way

But like a nun, she'd none of love
She could not be seduced
For she had Him who reigned above
And more, she had St Just.
St Just had been a vampire long
Before my father's birth
And where he went came Hell along
To burn the cursed earth
He made his way, his pack in tow
From town to wretched town
He spread them wide and laid them low
And, laughing, burned them down
And word throughout the village spread
As I'd already learned
The neighb'ring towns lay bathed in red
St Just had this way turned

INRI
They huddled in the dark'ning church
Their terrors running wild
Til softly, from his stony perch
The Reverend Father smiled
The shepherd does not leave behind
the lamb that tiring, falls
And God is good, and God is kind
He will protect these walls

The walls withstood St Just, it's true
He could not smash them in

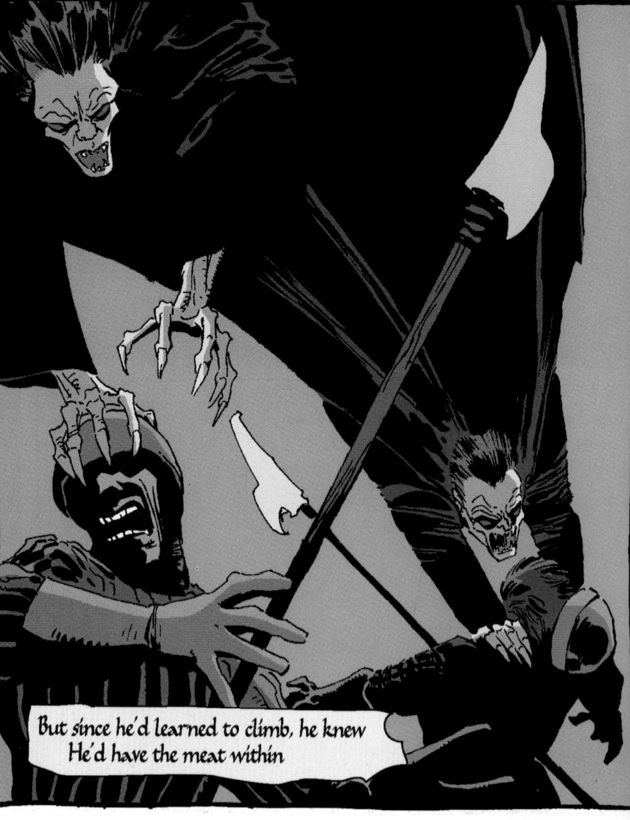
But since he'd learned to climb, he knew
He'd have the meat within

It started by the eastern gate
One family, still abed
Their child cried out for help -- too late
And fear like fire spread
"To arms!" the men were called, but none
Was man enough to fight

In St Just's way there stood but one
One maiden, dressed in white.

And those that dared to look that night
A glorious tale could tell

The girl who faced the devil's might
And sent him back to Hell

His brothers, hissing, vengeance vowed
As from the town they fled
"We'll break you, girl! We'll see you cowed!"

"Please try"
Was all she said

And so the gates were shut upon the creatures of the night
But still the danger was not gone

Still all was not yet right

"Beware!" intoned the wild-eyed Priest
His voice at fever pitch
"A vampire is a heinous beast
But worse yet..

"...is a witch!"
"That girl has power like none before
'Tis evil, by Saint Paul
She walks with Darkness, Satan's whore
She's here to damn us all!"

"There's but one way to save this town
And please our heav'nly sire
To bring that wanton woman down"

"And purge her soul with fire!"
For most, it does not last so long
The smoke their breath will take
But she was strong, so very stong
She burned up wide awake
I brought her this, this great reward
With talk of Destiny

She cried out, "Father! Help me, Lord!"
But kept her eyes on me.

The town made merry, gamboled, dined
They'd nothing now to fear

They burned the darkness from my mind
The world at last was clear
For God is good...
And God is kind...
But He's not welcome here.
TS
·01·

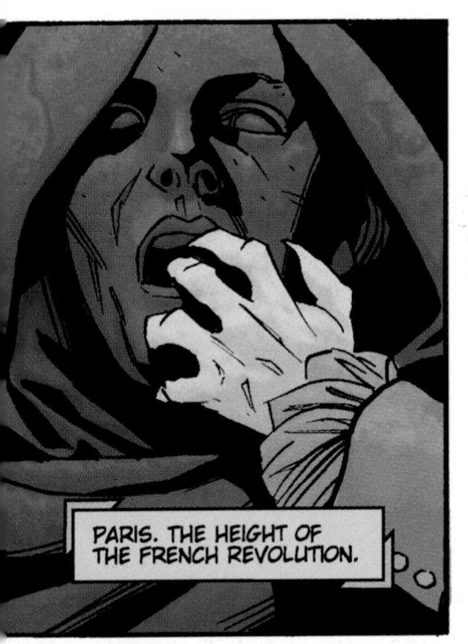
PARIS. THE HEIGHT OF THE FRENCH REVOLUTION.

EVIL JUST DOESN'T WANT TO DIE. NO MATTER HOW MANY TIMES YOU TRY AND KILL IT...

JEAN!!!
MERDE!!!
The Innocent

SPHLAT!!!

DIE, YOU BASTARD !
NO!! S'IL VOUS PLAIT!!!
CLAUDINE? MON AMOUR ...
ARE YOU ALL RIGHT?
I'M FINE. TIRED, BUT FINE.
ATTENDEZ--
I HAVE THE INFORMATION. THE NEXT VAMPIRE ...
AN ARISTOCRATIC TYRANT WHO FEEDS FROM THE POOR IN ORDER TO SLAKE HIS UNNATURAL THIRST.
WHERE?

I WILL TAKE YOU THERE ...

BUT LET THE NIGHT SETTLE A LITTLE WHILE FIRST ...

"IN A SUITE OF APARTMENTS ON THE RUE ST. DENIS IS WHERE HE HIDES.
"FIND HIM.
"DESTROY HIM.
"GOOD LUCK."

CRRREE-EEE-KKK....

YOU FILTH ... IN MY HOUSE ...!

NO!!!!

PLEASE ... NOT THE CHILDREN...
NO!!!!! NOOOO-OOOOO!!!
MURDERER!! MURDERER
UMMMPHF...
NO... NO... NO...

YOU LIED TO ME. I LOVED YOU AND YOU LIED TO ME, YOU BASTARD.

HE WAS AN ARISTOCRATIC PIG WHO DESERVED TO DIE. THEY ALL DESERVE TO DIE. THEY HIDE FROM MADAME GUILLOTINE, BUT I WILL FIND THEM AND SEND MY ANGEL OF DEATH TO DESTROY THEM.

YOU MADE ME
... A KILLER. A
COLD-BLOODED
MURDERER.

PPPFHH!

EVIL JUST DOESN'T WANT TO DIE. NO MATTER HOW MANY TIMES YOU TRY AND KILL IT.

THE MORE YOU TRY, THE MORE YOU SEE IT ALL AROUND YOU. IN THE FACES OF EVERYONE -- THE PEOPLE YOU LOVE, THE PEOPLE YOU TRUST...
... IN YOUR OWN REFLECTION ...

HOW DO YOU FIGHT THAT?
HOW CAN WE ... EVER ...
The End

SHOULD IT EVER BECOME NECESSARY OR DESIRABLE TO VANQUISH FROM A YOUNG WOMAN'S HEAD EVERY SENSIBLE NOTION AND AIM, KNOW THIS: THAT THE SUREST METHOD IS TO ANNOUNCE THAT THE LARGEST HOUSEHOLD IN HER SMALL NEIGHBORHOOD INTENDS TO HOLD A BALL.

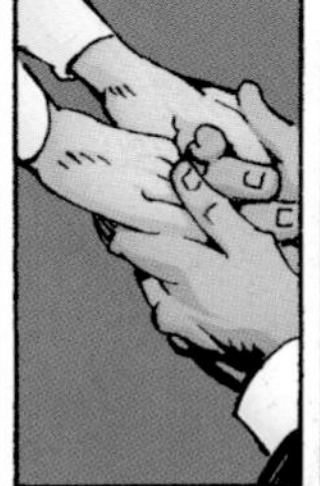

Presumption

CATHERINE, DEAR SISTER, YOU HAVE BEEN SO THOUGHTFUL AND LOW LATELY. WON'T YOU ALLOW EVEN THESE FESTIVITIES TO BRING YOU CHEER?

I WILL TRY.

DOES FATE EVER RING A BELL WHEN A CERTAIN TWO YOUNG PEOPLE ARE BROUGHT TOGETHER? PERHAPS NOT, BUT SURELY AN AUTHOR MAY.

CONSIDER THE PEAL RUNG.

ONLY ONE LADY HERE, AS SHE BEGINS THE DANCE, FEELS THE COLD HAND OF THE GRAVE ON HERS AND KNOWS WHAT IT IS SHE FEELS.

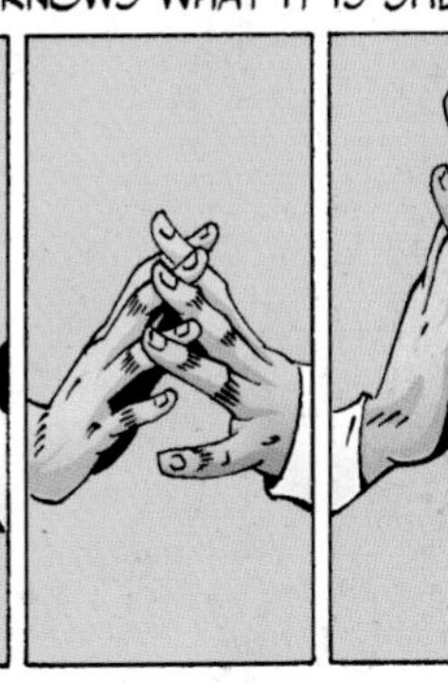

IT IS NEWS OF GREAT IMPORT TO LEARN IF AND WHAT YOU HUNT . . .
. . . HOW MUCH YOU LIKE OR DISLIKE MODERN POEMS . . .
. . . EVEN IF YOU PREFER A RAGOUT OR A FRICASSEE--
!

I SEE MANY YOUNG GIRLS HERE. IS THIS HOW THEY ALL FILL THEIR HOURS? WITH IDLE SPECULATION AND MEAN ARTS?

OR IS THIS PERHAPS PECULIAR TO YOU?

YOU ARE HARSH INDEED, SIR. YOUR RESENTMENT SEEMS OVERLARGE.
NOW, WE ARE TANGLING THE OTHERS. WE SHOULD STEP AWAY.

I DON'T LIKE BEING THE OBJECT OF SCRUTINY. IT IS UNCOMFORTABLE.
THAT'S NOT WHAT I MEAN.
THEN PERHAPS YOU SHOULD NOT STOP DANCING HALFWAY THROUGH THE MUSIC.

I DO NOT LIKE THINKING THAT EVERY WOMAN IS WATCHING ME.

THEN YOU ARE CORRECT TO FROWN UPON ME FOR DARING TO BRING IT TO YOUR ATTENTION.

A TERRIBLE SIN INDEED.

IT WAS A STRANGE START. THE SLAYER AND THE VAMPIRE PARTED UNCOMFORTABLY. . .

IT WAS JUST AS WELL, THE SLAYER MUSED. IT WOULD DO NO ONE ANY GOOD TO LIKE THE CREATURE ONE WAS DESTINED TO DESTROY... IT IS AN UNSKILLED SOLDIER INDEED THAT CANNOT WORK UP AT LEAST A GOOD HEALTHY DISLIKE FOR THE ENEMY.

I SAW. EVERYONE SAW.
WHY DID HE STOP DANCING AND COME OVER SO COLD AND ANGRY?
HE WAS VERY SILENT AT THE END.
OH YES, I'VE LEARNED SOMETHING IMPORTANT ABOUT OUR MR. WESTON...
HE IS A MAN WHO STRIVES TO LOOK AND BEHAVE THE BEST OF ANY MAN IN THE ROOM, THEN RESENTS IT WHEN HIS CARES DRAW THE ATTENTION THEY SEEK.
AN UNPLEASANT MIX OF PRESUMPTION AND RESENTMENT.
I CAN SEE HIM IN THE CARD ROOM, THERE. DO YOU NOT WISH YOU KNEW WHAT HE WAS SAYING TO HIS BROTHER?
WITH WHAT WEAPON DOES SUCH A BEAUTIFUL LADY STRIKE YOU SILENT, EDWARD? I THOUGHT FOR A MOMENT YOU HAD SINGLED HER OUT AS A LIKELY TARGET, BUT NOW YOU BACK AWAY.
I DO NOT BACK AWAY.
I RECONSIDER MY APPROACH.
THE SLAYER AND HER PREY CANNOT STAY APART FOR LONG. THIS STORY HAS NOT THE CAPACITY TO SUPPORT LONG ESTRANGEMENTS...
ALLOW ME.
YOU SPEAK.
ON OCCASION.
TELL ME, ARE YOU ALWAYS SO FREE IN SPEAKING WITH MEN NEW TO YOUR ACQUAINTANCE?

I SEE NO POINT IN WAITING UNTIL I HAVE MADE A FRIEND TO INSULT HIM. IN FACT, I WOULD RATHER NOT INSULT A FRIEND. THUS I AM REQUIRED TO ACT QUICKLY.
YOU ARE FREE WITH YOUR WORDS INDEED.
OUR SOCIETY AFFORDS WOMEN FEW FREEDOMS EXCEPT THE ABILITY TO LEARN ALL SHE CAN AND SPEAK ALL SHE MAY GET AWAY WITH. I'D BE FOOLISH TO NEGLECT SUCH SMALL OPTIONS.
YOU FIND THE LIFE OF A LADY CONFINING?
PERHAPS THEN YOU'LL CONSIDER A SMALL...
...CHALLENGE.
THE TERRACE. OFF-LIMITS TO AN UNMARRIED LADY AND GENTLEMAN DURING A BALL. YOU CLAIM THAT YOU CHAFE FOR FREEDOM. HOW MUCH DO YOU WANT IT?
A HAPPY MOMENT IT IS WHEN DUTY AND DESIRE BOTH LEAD OUT THE SAME TERRACE DOOR.

CATHERINE WAS A VAMPIRE. BUT SHE WAS RIGHT. THE LIFE OF A LADY OFFERS MANY LIMITATIONS...
DID YOU GET HER, MISS ELIZABETH?
EDWARD. ALWAYS, EDWARD.
P.C.R.-48

THOSE LIMITATIONS WERE WHY THE SLAYER HAD GIVEN UP THE LIFE OF A WOMAN YEARS BEFORE.
TO LIVE AS A FREE WOMAN, MISS ELIZABETH WESTON HAD TO LIVE AS A MAN.
I WILL NOT SAY SHE LIVED FOREVER, NOR EVEN LONG.

BUT WHILE SHE LIVED, THE ASSUMPTIONS OF OTHERS PROTECTED HER, AS A COAT THICKER THAN CLOTH.

DREAMS AND REGRETS DWELL FAR BENEATH. AND REALLY...

WHO ARE WE TO GUESS AT THOSE?

"The Navajo tell of a time in 'the great before'... when the land bounded by the sacred mountains was barren, arid...
"...dead...

"An unholy place... Full of dark spirits, beasts...

"...demons...

" And it was here, into this realm, the Twins were sent...
"To' Bájishchíní.. Born for Water... to prepare the earth, make it fertile...

"And the other... the one called Naayéé'neizghání...

"Monster Slayer.

"To make it safe for the People... the Diné... to emerge from the three previous underworlds into this... the Fourth World..."

...the Glittering World

CARPENTRY
♫ MEET ME TO-NIGHT, DARLIN', DOWN BY THE GATE...

♪ ...ANXIOUSLY, LONGINGLY, FOR THEE I'LL WAIT...

...THERE, WHILE THE LADY MOON SOFTLY RECLINES... ♫

THERE WHILE HER BEAMIN' EYES LOVINGLY SHINE... ♫

WILLY'S
...IN SWEETEST ♫ ♪ DREAMS, HAPPY, I'LL WAIT...

...EAGER TO MEET YE, DARLIN' DOWN BY THE GAT
SSKWEEEUURRRK

GA-LUMP GA-L

LOOKING FOR A VAMPIRE.
THAT A FACT? WELP, AIN'T SEEN ANY 'ROUND HERE.
Snort!

MAYBE, MY PARTNER 'N ME CAN HELP YA LOOK ARC-UHH!

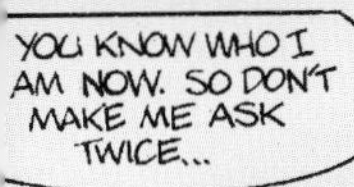
YOU KNOW WHO I AM NOW. SO DON'T MAKE ME ASK TWICE...

WHERE IS SHE?

UP-UPSTAIRS.

YOUR HUNT IS OVER, LITTLE SLAYER.

YOU HAVE FOUND ME.

UNFORTUNATELY FOR YOU.

YOU KNEW I'D NEVER STOP LOOKING, TO.
YOU KILLED MY WATCHER.
ONE LESS WHITE MAN.

LIKE YOUR FATHER?

FATHER...
YOU MEAN THE CAVALRY SCUM WHO POISONED MY MOTHER WITH HIS SEED! MIXING MY BLOOD...
DAMNING ME TO NEVER FEEL A PART OF EITHER WORLD...NEVER BELONGING...
BUT THEN YOU, OF ALL, KNOW HOW THAT FEELS, DON'T YOU, LITTLE SLAYER?
NOT DINE... NOR DEMON...
THIS GLITTERING WORLD IS NO MORE YOURS THAN IT WAS MINE...

BUT UNLIKE YOU, I BELONG TO A WORLD NOW, ONE WHERE NO DISTINCTIONS ARE MADE. THERE IS ONLY US...
AND FOOD.

"The Navajos tell of a time in 'the great before'...
"When the one called Monster Slayer came upon Death hiding by the side of the road...
"Death begged Monster Slayer to spare him.
"'Think of the suffering of the old ones,' he pleaded.
"'And the unborn generations...'

"Monster Slayer thought long about Death's warning...

"And in the end...

"...it was decided...

"...that Death...

"...would go on."
"BOY GOLLY, YOU SURE KNOW HOW TO' SPIN A HECK OF A YARN THERE, PADRE!"

VAMPIRES... MONSTER SLAYERS... YESSIR, A HECK OF A YARN.
Forgive me, my son. But as you'll be building a new town on this land, I thought you should know its accursed history.
APPRECIATE THAT, PADRE. I SURELY DO. BUT I'M MUCH MORE INTERESTED IN ITS FUTURE.
Do you have any idea what you'll be calling your new town, Mr...?
WILKENS. RICHARD WILKENS. SOMETHING REAL CHEERY SOUNDING. I WAS THINKING... HAPPYDALE.
OR SUNNY ACRES. WHAT DO YOU THINK?
THE END

THE END OF MY FOURTEENTH YEAR WAS A STRANGE TIME.
ONE MINUTE, I FELT LIKE I WAS ALMOST AN ADULT, LIKE I WAS JUST ABOUT TO BLOOM AND UNDERSTAND EVERYTHING IN THE WORLD.
AND THE NEXT MINUTE I WAS STILL A KID WHO MISSED MY FATHER AND WANTED A BICYCLE AND SECRETLY KISSED MY PILLOW PRETENDING IT WAS A BOY.
TROMP
TROMP
TROMP
SOMETIMES I QUESTIONED CERTAIN THINGS, BUT THEN I REMEMBERED I WAS JUST A GIRL WITH DIRTY FINGER-NAILS AND A LOW MARK IN SEWING CLASS.
TROMP! TROMP! TROMP!
AND THEN I WAS GLAD TO BE A PART OF SOMETHING BIGGER THAN MYSELF. I WAS GLAD NOT TO BE ALONE.
TROMP!
TROMP!
TROMP!

NUREMBERG, GERMANY. SEPTEMBER 10, 1938.
YOU MUST BECOME AS TOUGH AS LEATHER, AS SWIFT AS GREYHOUNDS, AND AS HARD AS KRUPP STEEL.
NEVER FORGET THAT ONE DAY YOU WILL RULE THE WORLD.
HEIL HITLER!
Sonnenblume

MOTHER DIDN'T TELL *ME* TO BUY BREAD.
FINE, KARL, I'LL DO IT MYSELF.
clip
Clop
Clip
Clop
RING-DING
FRESH FROM THE OVEN. FOR YOU, SONNENBLUME, JUST 40 PFENNIGS. AND HERE'S YOUR DEAR MOTHER'S ROLLING PIN. SHE'S A GREAT COOK, YOUR MOTHER.
SHE ALWAYS SAYS YOU'RE THE BEST BAKER IN NUREMBERG.
DADDY, I WANT TO WEAR AN OUTFIT LIKE SONNEN-BLUME'S SOMEDAY.
GO HOME, ANNI.
clip
clop
clip
clop
BEING ALONE CAN BE SCARY.

TODAY GERMANY LISTENS TO US AND TOMORROW, THE WORLD--
SONNENBLUME?
HOW ARE YOU, MY LITTLE SONNENBLUME? YOUR BIRTHDAY'S JUST AROUND THE BEND FROM NOW. WILL IT BE A CHOCOLATE CAKE THIS YEAR?
YOU'RE FRIENDS WITH HER?
YOU KNOW HER?
WE USED TO BUY BREAD FROM HER, THAT'S ALL.
YOU'RE DISGUSTING!
WHAT'S WRONG WITH YOU ANNI?
HA HA HA HA HA HA HA HA
I'D RATHER EAT SHOES THAN EAT SOMETHING YOU BAKED, YOU DIRTY JEWESS!

BLOW OUT THE CANDLES DEAR.
YEAH, WHAT'S THE MATTER WITH YOU, ANNI?
THIS TASTES LIKE OLD SHOES.
HANNAH STEINGOTT BAKED THAT CAKE. SHE'S A GOOD GERMAN WOMAN.
STILL TASTES LIKE SHOES. AND SOUR ONES AT THAT. I'VE GOT TO GO. I HAVE A MEETING.
I HAD TO GO TOO.
I PATROLLED ALL NIGHT. THINKING.
Clop
Clip
Clip
Clop
ELSOHN
AND THEN I SAW SOMETHING.

NOVEMBER 9, 1938.
WHOO-HOO! WHOO-HOO!
GET IN THERE.
PLEASE, NO!
HA HA HA-HA-HA HA HA
WHY DON'T YOU PRAY NOW, OLD MAN?
MAYBE THIS WILL TEACH YOU FOR NOT SHAVING YOUR FACE.
HA HA HA HA
AAAAAA!

NO ONE WILL HELP YOU, OLD MAN. YOU'RE ALL ALONE.
YOU ANIMALS, LET GO OF HIM!
SHE CALLS US ANIMALS?
HA HA HA HA HA HA HA HA HA HA HA HA HA HA HA HA
ENOUGH JOKES. GET THE JEWS AND LOAD THEM IN THE TRUCK.
I DON'T KNOW WHERE THEY WENT.
I KNOW.
AND I KNOW WHAT I HAVE TO DO.
I HAVE TO DO MY DUTY.

YOU. DID YOU SEE THE JEWS?
THE BEARDED MAN AND HIS FAMILY. DO YOU KNOW WHERE THEY ARE?
YES.
CRACK
IT'S MY DUTY TO FIGHT EVIL.
AND I FINALLY RECOGNIZE THE REAL EVIL HERE. AND NOW I WILL FIGHT IT. NOW I WILL BEGIN.
BECAUSE I CAN'T BE LIKE EVERYONE ELSE.
HELLO? MR. GREEN, MRS. GREEN, SARAH?
IT'S OKAY. IT'S JUST ME.
clip clop clip clop
SONNENBLUME...
the end

HARLEM SUNRISE. BEAUTIFUL. LI'S MY MAN. HE'S A COP. THIS MORNING HE RUINS EVERYTHING.
Gene Colan

HE WAKES UP.
Nikki Goes Down!

LI DOESN'T TELL ME HE'S ON STAKEOUT. I FIND OUT ANYWAY.
I FOLLOW.
HE DOESN'T KNOW I'M THE SLAYER.
HELL, HE DOESN'T KNOW WHAT A SLAYER IS. WE HAVE TO TALK. BUT NOT TONIGHT.

HE GOES FIRST.
FREEZE!
HE ALWAYS GOES FIRST.
LE BANC. GLAD I TAGGED ALONG.
THE BIG MAN'S SMUGGLING.
BUT NOT DRUGS.

LI'S TEAM'S THE BEST IN THE CITY.
GOOD COPS.
THEY'VE GOT WIVES. KIDS.

I HIT THE GROUND IN UNDER TWO SECONDS.
NOT SOON ENOUGH.
I DO WHAT I DO.
HOPING LI CAN HANDLE HIMSELF.
WHEN SOMETHING TOO BIG HAPPENS TOO FAST.

I FIGHT THE DARKNESS.
LI NEEDS ...
... ME. JUST LIKE I ...

... NEEDED HIM.
HOLD IT RIGHT THERE, SWEETHEART.
NEW YORK'S FINEST.
I SAID HOLD IT!
THEY'LL WANT ANSWERS.
SO WILL I.

MY MAN IS DEAD.
I DON'T FEEL A THING.
SPEND THE DAY BEATING INFORMATION OUT OF ANYTHING THAT WALKS, CRAWLS, OR SLITHERS.
THEY ALL POINT ME IN THE SAME DIRECTION.
TO THE TOP.
LE BANC'S HAVING A PARTY.

SO I WEAR PEARLS.
LE BANC UNVEILS HIS CARGO. A PREHISTORIC NIGHTMARE HUNTED DOWN FROM SOME DARK CORNER OF THE WORLD, AND BROUGHT TO MANHATTAN TO TERRIFY ANEW.
HELL WITH THAT.
MY MOM ALWAYS SAID, "IF YOU'RE GONNA FIGHT, FIGHT OUTSIDE."

I'VE GOT THIS CONDITION. FORGET THE NAME. BASICALLY? FEAR OF HEIGHTS.
IT TAKES ME HIGHER.

I CAN'T
BREATHE.
CAN BARELY
THINK.
PEARLS.
WHATEVER
WORKS.
TO
BRING
US
DOWN ...

THIS THING OWNS THE SKY.
BUT THE STREETS ARE MINE.
I GET AN IDEA.

RED CIRCLE
NO. 1 LINE
NEVER SAID IT WAS A GOOD ONE.
ONLY ONE I GOT.

SPRING IN HARLEM COMES AND GOES. BAHAMAS SUMMER BEGINS. HUNTING SEASON.
LE BANC'S MEN HAVE SPOTTED ANOTHER NEST. HE'S GOT BUSINESS TO FINISH.
SO DO I.
THE END

THIS ISN'T GOING GREAT.
TALES
I KNOW WHY, TOO.
THESE GUYS ARE OLD. EDUCATED.
THEY KNOW ALL THE SLAYER'S MOVES.
MY ADVANTAGE?

I DON'T KNOW ANY OF 'EM.
IT'S GOOD.
MAKES ME SPECIAL.

EVERY SLAYER SUBCONSCIOUSLY INHERITS THE MEMORIES OF ALL THE PREVIOUS SLAYERS.

'CEPT ME.
SPECIAL ME.

I DIDN'T EVEN KNOW THEY WERE CALLED "VAMPIRES" 'TIL I GOT TOLD.
I KNOW I'M SUPPOSED TO FIGHT 'EM; I'M THE ONLY ONE IN THE WORLD WHO CAN.
THE ONLY ONE.

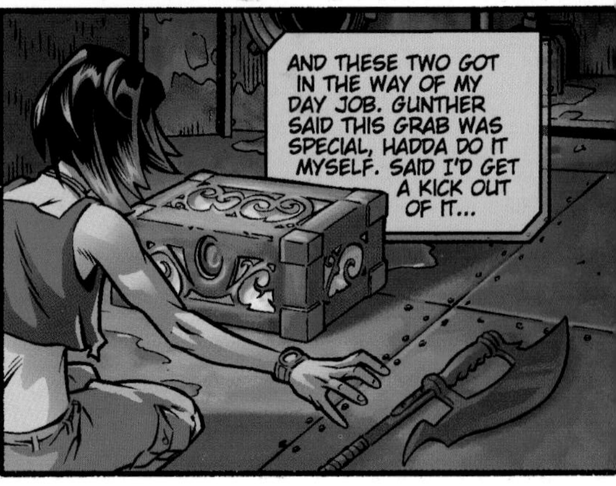
AND THESE TWO GOT IN THE WAY OF MY DAY JOB. GUNTHER SAID THIS GRAB WAS SPECIAL, HADDA DO IT MYSELF. SAID I'D GET A KICK OUT OF IT...

SCREEVUL EEP HOWOWOK SLAYER MEK MEK SLAYEEVUL

TEK MU HEH HEH BYE
HEY!

THING IS NOT HUMAN. ACTUAL DEMON OF SOME KIND. STUCK IN THAT BOX FOR WHO KNOWS HOW LONG...
GIMME THAT BACK!
AND THE CREEP RECOGNIZED MY SCYTHE.

OH NO YOU--

DON'T ...
YENHA YENHA SCREEFALL BIM
NO WAY. NO WAY. THAT SCYTHE IS MY ONLY CONNECTION TO THE WHOLE SLAYER HERITAGE THING. AND IT KILLS GREAT.
ME MO
SO NO WAY IS SPIDER-MONKEY KEEPING THAT THING. HE WANTS TO RUN? FINE.
I CAN KEEP THAT UP ALL DAY.

HEART ... EXPLODING ...
SPIDER-MONKEY ... MUST DIE ...

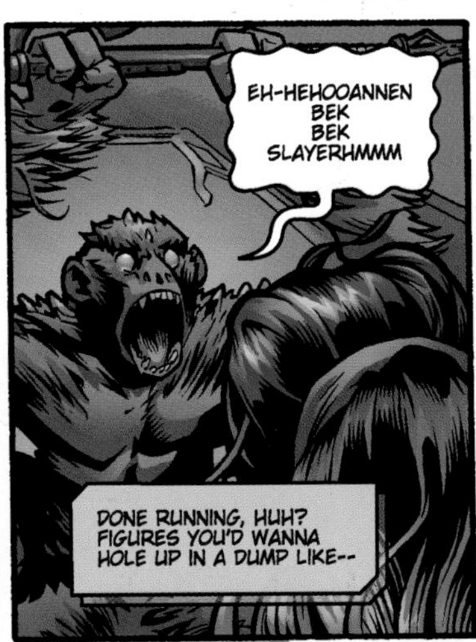
EH-HEHOOANNEN BEK BEK SLAYERHMMM
DONE RUNNING, HUH? FIGURES YOU'D WANNA HOLE UP IN A DUMP LIKE--

WATCHERS DIARY

IT'S ALL HERE ...

THE BATTLES, THE TRICKS ... THE FEARS AND THE VICTORIES ... ALL THE GIRLS, SO DIFFERENT, WHO LIVED AS I DO...
ALL OF THEIR STORIES ARE LAID BEFORE ME AND I ... MY HANDS ARE SHAKING.
I AM THE ONLY ONE IN THE WORLD...

... BUT I AM NOT ALONE.
THE END

PROLOGUE

story by
JOSS WHEDON
pencils by
LEINIL FRANCIS YU
inks by
DEXTER VINES
colors by
DAVE STEWART
letters by
MICHELLE MADSEN

RIGHTEOUS

story by
JOSS WHEDON
art by
TIM SALE
colors by
LEE LOUGHRIDGE
letters by
RICHARD STARKINGS

THE INNOCENT

story by
AMBER BENSON
art by
TED NAIFEH
colors by
DAVE STEWART
letters by
MICHELLE MADSEN

PRESUMPTION

story by
JANE ESPENSON
art by
P. CRAIG RUSSELL
colors by
LOVERN KINDZIERSKI
letters by
GALEN SHOWMAN

THE GLITTERING WORLD

story by
DAVID FURY
art and letters by
STEVE LIEBER
colors by
MATTHEW HOLLINGSWORTH

SONNENBLUME

story by
REBECCA RAND KIRSHNER
art and colors by
MIRA FRIEDMANN
letters by
JASON HVAM

NIKKI GOES DOWN!

story by
DOUG PETRIE
art by
GENE COLAN
colors by
DAVE STEWART
letters by
MICHELLE MADSEN

TALES

story by
JOSS WHEDON
pencils by
KARL MOLINE
inks by
ANDY OWENS
colors by
DAVE STEWART
letters by
MICHELLE MADSEN

publisher
MIKE RICHARDSON

editor
SCOTT ALLIE

assistant editor
MICHAEL CARRIGLITTO

book designer
DARCY HOCKETT

art director
MARK COX

cover art
TIM SALE

cover colors
LEE LOUGHRIDGE

special thanks to
BRETT MATTHEWS, CAROLINE KALLAS,
and GEORGE SNYDER *at* BUFFY THE VAMPIRE SLAYER
and DEBBIE OLSHAN *at* FOX LICENSING.

based on the television series BUFFY THE VAMPIRE SLAYER,
created by JOSS WHEDON

PUBLISHED BY
DARK HORSE BOOKS
A DIVISION OF
DARK HORSE COMICS, INC.
10956 SE MAIN STREET
MILWAUKIE, OR 97222

FIRST EDITION: NOVEMBER 2001
ISBN 10: 1-56971-605-6
ISBN 13: 978-1-56971-605-2

5 7 9 10 8 6

PRINTED IN CHINA

ALSO FROM JOSS WHEDON

SERENITY

Joss Whedon, Brett Matthews, Will Conrad, and Laura Martin

The ragtag crew of *Serenity* take on a scavenger mission with the hopes of earning enough dough to disappear for a while. Only too late do they realize the whole gig is orchestrated by an old enemy eager to remake their acquaintance with the help of some covert-operatives known only as the Blue Gloves.

$9.95, ISBN: 1-59307-449-2

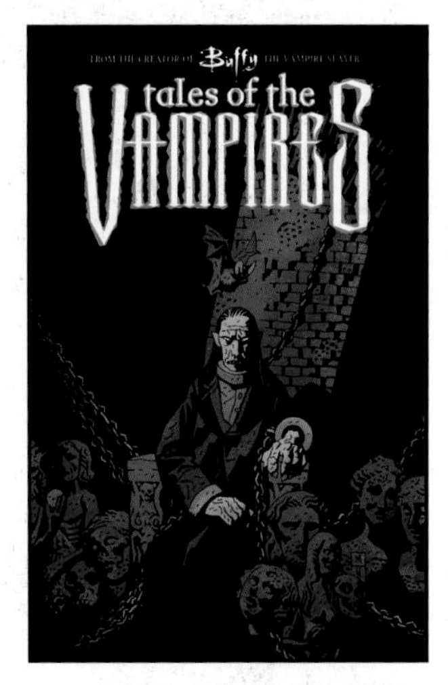

BUFFY THE VAMPIRE SLAYER: TALES OF THE VAMPIRES

Joss Whedon, Brett Matthews, Cameron Stewart, Tim Sale, and others

The creator of *Buffy the Vampire Slayer* reunites with the writers from his hit TV shows for a frightening look into the history of vampires. Illustrated by some of comics' greatest artists, the stories span medieval times to today, including Buffy's rematch with Dracula, and Angel's ongoing battle with his own demons.

$15.95, ISBN: 1-56971-749-4

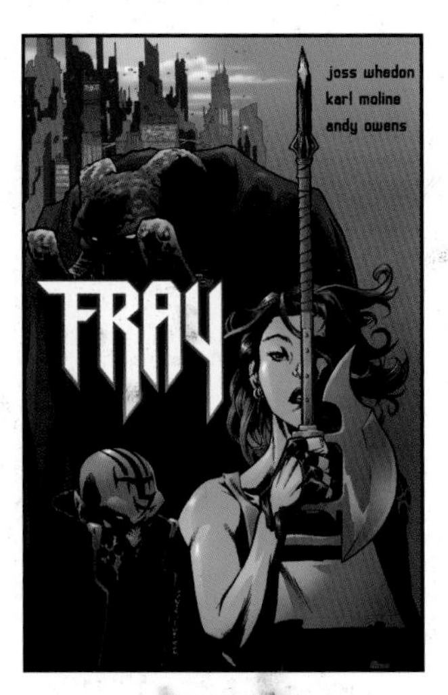

FRAY TPB

Joss Whedon, Karl Moline, Andy Owens, and Dave Stewart

In a future Manhattan so poisoned it doesn't notice the monsters on its streets, it's up to a gutter-punk named Fray to unite a fallen city against a demonic plot to consume mankind. But will this girl who thought she had no future embrace her destiny—as the first Vampire Slayer in centuries—in time?

$19.95, ISBN: 1-56971-751-6

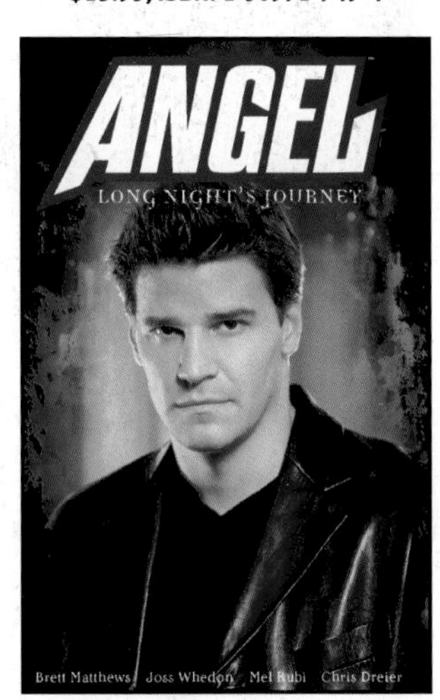

ANGEL: LONG NIGHT'S JOURNEY

Joss Whedon, Brett Matthews, and Mel Rubi

An enemy from Angel's past has come to L.A. Now, in one catastrophic night, Angel must go toe-to-toe with three of the most powerful monsters he has ever faced. Together, Brett Matthews and *Angel* creator Joss Whedon retool and reinvent Angel, crafting a story so big it wouldn't fit on the small screen.

$12.95, ISBN: 1-56971-752-4

AVAILABLE AT YOUR LOCAL COMICS SHOP OR BOOKSTORE

To find a comics shop in your area, call 1-888-266-4226

For more information or to order direct visit darkhorse.com or call 1-800-862-0052 • Mon.-Fri. 9 A.M. to 5 P.M. Pacific Time

***Prices and availability subject to change without notice**

ALSO FROM DARK HORSE BOOKS

BUFFY THE VAMPIRE SLAYER: HAUNTED
Jane Espenson and Cliff Richards

A body-snatching, blood-sucking poltergeist stirs amidst the charred rubble of what used to be Sunnydale High and Buffy's left to face it armed only with an enigmatic message from Faith: "You're already dead." Don't miss Jane Espenson, long-time writer for the Buffy TV series, bring you the first appearance of Faith in comics.

$12.95, ISBN: 1-56971-737-0

BUFFY THE VAMPIRE SLAYER: RING OF FIRE
Doug Petrie and Ryan Sook

An apocalypse is brewing over the Hellmouth. Someone has stolen a set of ancient samurai armor from a cargo ship with the hope of reviving its demonic owner. How will Buffy stand against this unspeakable evil now that Angel has teamed with Spike and Dru and returned to his murderous ways?

$9.95, ISBN: 1-56971-482-7

DAMN NATION
Andrew Cosby and J. Alexander

Overrun by a vampire plague, the United States is quarantined from the world. When scientists trapped inside the US discover a cure, it's up to a Special Ops team from the President's current offices in London to go get it. Yet, not everyone on earth wants to see America cured.

$12.95, ISBN: 1-59307-389-5

THE DARK HORSE BOOK OF HAUNTINGS
Mike Mignola, P. Craig Russell, Paul Chadwick, Evan Dorkin, Jill Thompson, Gary Gianni and others

Hellboy discovers an unexpected connection to the spirits in a hidden cellar, a boy and his family vanish into an abandoned house, and a few good pups solve the mystery of a haunted doghouse. All this and more await you in this hardcover collection of original horror stories by comic's top talent.

$14.95, ISBN: 1-56971-958-6

AVAILABLE AT YOUR LOCAL COMICS SHOP OR BOOKSTORE
To find a comics shop in your area, call 1-888-266-4226
For more information or to order direct visit darkhorse.com or call 1-800-862-0052 • Mon.-Fri. 9 A.M. to 5 P.M. Pacific Time
***Prices and availability subject to change without notice**